SMELLY'S PARTY

Not Smelly. Smally! You got it wrong by mistake.

an Action Animals production

SMALLY THE MOUSE

and friends (who don't like him)

in...

SMALLY'S PARTY

cleverly written and drawn by Daren King

BLOOMSBURY

First published in Great Britain in 2005

Copyright © 2005 by Daren King

The moral right of the author has been asserted

Bloomsbury Publishing Plc, 36 Soho Square, London W1D 3QY

A CIP catalogue record for this book is available from the British Library

ISBN 0 7475 7903 2
ISBN-13 9780747579038

10 9 8 7 6 5 4 3 2 1

Printed in Singapore by Tien Wah Press

All papers used by Bloomsbury Publishing are natural, recyclable products made from wood grown in well-managed forests.
The manufacturing processes conform to the environmental regulations of the country of origin.

http://www.bloomsbury.com

http://www.darenking.co.uk
http://www.actionanimals.co.uk

Who's that tiny mouse? He's even smaller than me!

I'm Smally the Mouse. Who are you?

I'm Smallier, the Even Smaller Mouse.

Will you buy me some sweets?

I don't think they make sweets in your size.

Oh no! It's Paula, the Sexually Available Female Hedgehog!

She's pretty, but she's too old for me. And she's spiky.

Hello, Paula!

Hello, Smally!

Smally, will you hold me? I haven't been held for so long.

What about when you were in prison for sexually assaulting a bull?

They only held me overnight.

I want to be crushed to your chest like a pink slutty flower!

I'm not in a good place right now, Paula.

I've been prickled once before!

Are you Two Hoots the Owl?

You know perfectly well who I am.
Why are you asking my name?

For the benefit of the reader.

Two Hoots, can I call you One Hoots instead?
I find Two Hoots difficult to say.

If you must. You little sod.

Maybe I won't then.

He doesn't look happy.

Hello! Is your name Peter?   No, why?

It's painted on your shell. A boy painted it. It's his name.

Then what's your name?

I don't have a name.

Names suggest meaning, and there is no meaning.

The universe is dead and names are stupid.

I will call you No Purpose Tortoise.

I don't care what you call me, as long as you don't ever call me.

I hope Paula doesn't come to my party. She's spiky.

Ah, so you are having a party! Yes. I mean, no. I mean, I don't know.

No Purpose Tortoise, will you come to my party?

Whether or not I attend your party is of no consequence.

What is a party but a herd of animals consuming intoxicants?

My parties aren't like that. My parties are fun.

There's going to be balloons.

What is a balloon but a bag of air?

On a string! Don't forget the string, or you can't hold it.

How are you, my feathered friend?   I'm not your friend.

Acquaintance then.

Nope.

Relative?

Hardly!

Our relationship is purely propinquitous!

Look it up in the dictionary, you little shit.

Will there be strippers at your party?

I won't get one then.   How can you have a party without strippers?

I could get a human stripper. A lady. With big boobs.

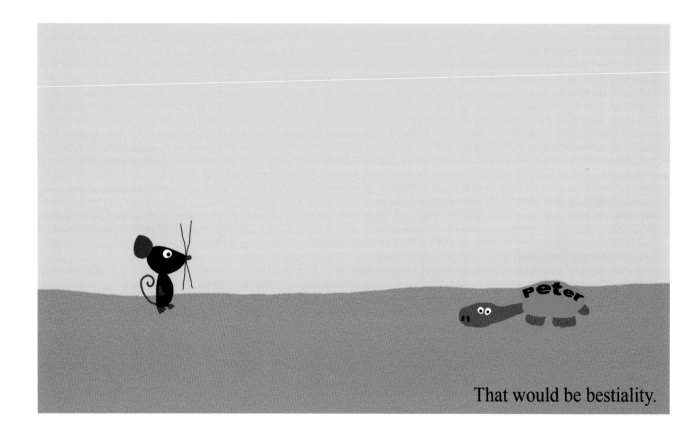

peter

That would be bestiality.

My party has begun! I hope my friends turn up.

knock!
knock!

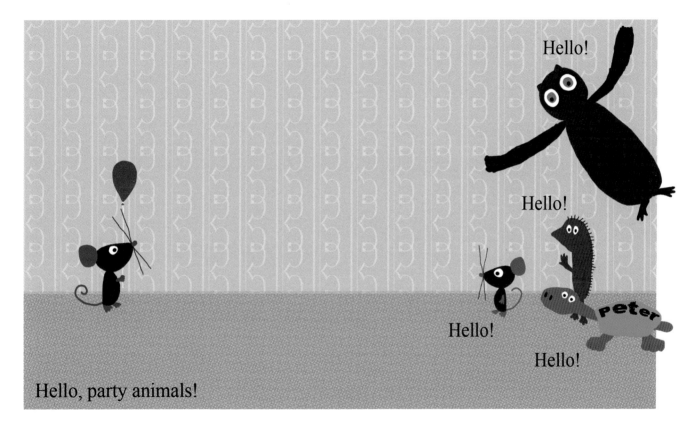

Hello!

Hello!

Hello!

Hello!

Hello, party animals!

What's that white powder, No Purpose Tortoise?

Gak.

Why do you call it gak?

Because...

It's dirty.

Are you enjoying the party, Two Hoots?

I'll say!

Why is your cigarette shaped like a trumpet?   It's full of drugs.

What does it do?

Makes you high. Have some.

I don't need drugs to get high.

I've got a balloon.

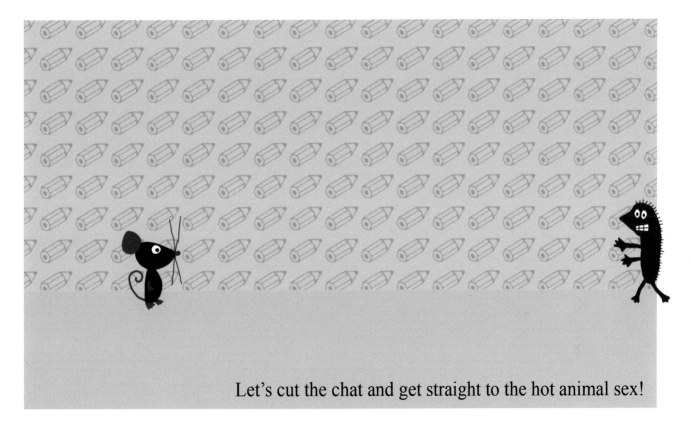

Let's cut the chat and get straight to the hot animal sex!

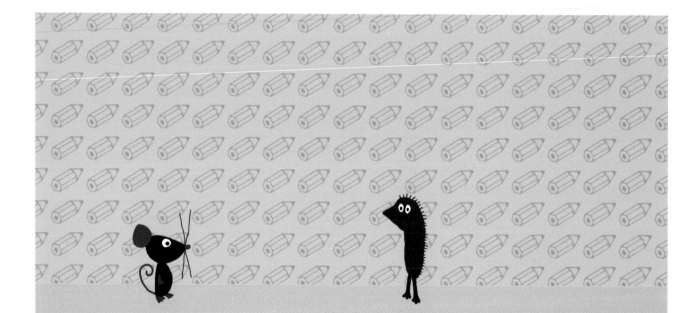

I'm not very good in bed, Paula. I'm too small.
I get lost among the sheets.

Sometimes, the next morning,
I get thrown in the laundry with the knickers and socks.

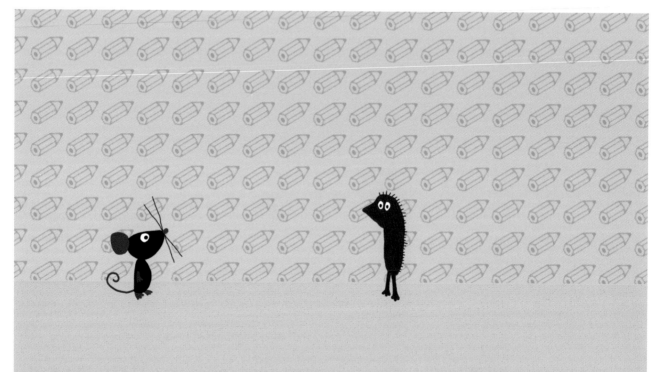

And what if I shrink in the wash? There won't be anything left!

Oi! Smallier!

Not you, Smally. You can cock off.

Go play with tractors.

Smallier, do you like sweets?

I love sweets! Have this one. I'm too old for sweets.

It's made of paper, Mr Hoots!

It's magic. Put it on your tongue.

Faster! Faster!

I can't do it faster. I'm a tortoise.

I hope you're wearing a condom, Peter. I have to think of my future.

There is no future. Only oblivion.

Pull it out and shoot it over my spikes.

Mr Hoots, that paper sweet made me feel funny.

What's happening, Mr Hoots?

Mr Hoots?

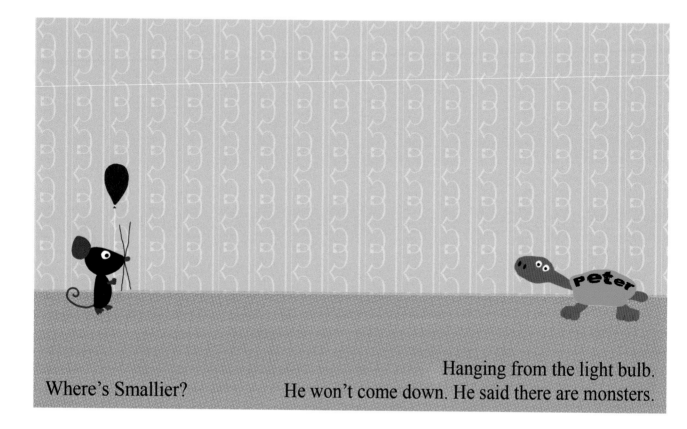

Where's Smaller?

Hanging from the light bulb.
He won't come down. He said there are monsters.

I gave him a tab of acid. I am pure feathered evil.

Drugs spoil parties. I will save the day with my nice balloon.

Thanks for making my party the best party in the whole world!